PINGU
annual 1996

£4.99
UK only

Contents

Written by Brenda Apsley
Illustrated by Jo Davies and Jane Swift
Edited by Nina Filipek

Published in Great Britain in 1995 by World International, an imprint of Egmont Publishing Ltd., Egmont House, PO Box 111, Great Ducie Street, Manchester M60 3BL.
Printed in Italy. ISBN 0 7498 2318 6

Pingu's photograph album

Hello! I'm Pingu, the penguin. I live in a cold, snowy place called the South Pole with my family and my friends. I took some photographs of them and put them in my album. Would you like to see it?

This is Papa. He has an important job. He delivers letters and parcels on his post sledge. Sometimes he lets me help him.

This is Mama.
She is very kind and looks after me and my sister.

Pinga is my baby sister — yes, the one with a potty on her head!

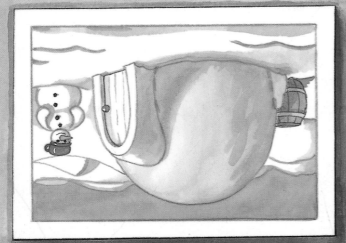

This is where me and my family live, in a house made from blocks of ice. It's called an igloo. Oops! I stuck the photograph in upside-down!

My grandpa lives in his own igloo not far from us. He is teaching me how to play the accordion. I'm not very good!

Robby the seal is my very best friend. He's a really good swimmer and we catch fish together.

Ping is another of my friends.
We both like ice skating.

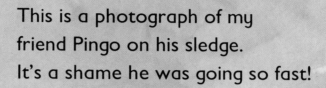

This is a photograph of my
friend Pingo on his sledge.
It's a shame he was going so fast!

Pingi is in my class at school.
She always wants to sit next
to me. It's embarrassing!

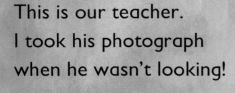

This is our teacher.
I took his photograph
when he wasn't looking!

What is different?

I took these two photographs of my family and my friends. There are 5 things that are different in the bottom photograph. Can you find them all?

The answers are on page 61.

The school orchestra

Ever since Grandpa started to teach Pingu how to play the accordion, Pingu has been very keen on music. He played so many records on the record player in the igloo that Mama had a good idea for a birthday present for him. She and Papa bought Pingu a little personal stereo with earpieces. Now Pingu could listen to music as loud as he liked without bothering anyone else. Pinga bought her brother a special belt to clip his stereo to.

One day Pingu and his friends were in school listening as their teacher explained about snowflakes. At least, Ping, Pingo and Pingi were listening to the teacher. Naughty Pingu had brought his personal stereo to school. He had his earpieces on, and was listening to music instead of the teacher!

"Now, can anyone tell me how many sides a snowflake has?" the teacher asked.

Three flippers shot into the air and three little voices said, "Me, Sir, I know!"

The teacher looked at his pupils. They were all looking at him. All except Pingu. He was gazing into the distance, his eyes half closed.

"Pingu, do you know the answer?" the teacher asked.

Pingu didn't hear him.

"Pingu, please pay attention!" said the teacher. "Do you know the answer or not?"

Pingu didn't hear him.

The teacher didn't look very pleased. "Pingu, please answer me at once! How many sides does a snowflake have?"

Pingu didn't answer the teacher. He didn't even look at him, even though Pingi nudged him hard.

The teacher walked to where Pingu was sitting. "Pingu, can you hear me?" he shouted.

Pingu couldn't.

The teacher looked hard at Pingu. Then, "Aha!" he said. "So that's it!" and pulled the earpieces out of Pingu's ears.

Pingu was in real trouble. He had to stay behind after school. The teacher made him write out 'A snowflake has six sides' twenty times.

When Pingu had finished the teacher said, "Do you have anything to say?"

Pingu hung his head. "I'm very sorry," he said. "It's just that Grandpa gave me a new music tape this morning, and I just couldn't wait to listen to it. I love music, I really do."

"Yes, I think you do," said the teacher, who had just had an idea. "How would you like to be in charge of a school orchestra?" he asked.

"Yes please!" said Pingu.

The teacher took a big box and put it on the desk. "There isn't any money for real instruments, but let's see if you can make your own. Here's a big box of bits and pieces to get you going."

At lunch time the next day Pingu and his friends didn't play snow football as they usually did. Instead they were very busy making musical instruments. They used the scrap box the teacher had given Pingu, and some things they had brought from home. They made a big bass drum from a dustbin lid, and stretched elastic bands across a biscuit tin lid to make a guitar. They filled yogurt pots with dried peas and beans to make shakers, and Robby gave them the skeleton of a huge fish. They played its bones with chopsticks, just like a xylophone. Pingu found that pan lids made very good cymbals.

Pingu and his friends went to Grandpa's house every afternoon after school to practise. They wouldn't let anyone else hear them, not even the teacher.

"How is the orchestra coming along?" the teacher asked Pingu one morning.

"Very well," said Pingu. He looked at his friends. "It is, isn't it?"

Ping, Pingo and Pingi all nodded their heads.

"Good," said the teacher, "because on Friday we are going to have a special meeting for parents after school, and I'd like you to play. Brothers and sisters can come along, too."

"Waark!" said Pingu. "Thank you, Sir!"

After school on Friday, Pingu and his friends sat with their instruments in a clearing at the side of the classroom. The audience sat on benches. Grandpa was the last to arrive, and sat beside Papa.

Papa looked at Grandpa. He was wearing the biggest pair of fluffy ear muffs that Papa had ever seen. "Pssst!" Papa whispered. "Why are you wearing ear muffs? It isn't very cold today."

Grandpa didn't say anything. He just smiled, and winked at Papa.

"Shhh!" said Mama. "The music is about to start."

Pingu bowed to the audience, then tapped a long fishbone on his music stand. "One, two, three!" he said, and the music began.

Pingo strummed his guitar, and crashed his pan lid cymbals together. Pingi played the fish skeleton xylophone and Ping hit the dustbin lid with two long fishbones. Pingu joined in too, waving his conducting stick enthusiastically.

The music was VERY loud, and there didn't seem to be much of a tune, but the orchestra members looked happy. Papa put his flippers over his ears and looked at Grandpa.

"Now I know why you put those big ear muffs on!" he said. "You've heard Pingu's orchestra before, haven't you?"

Grandpa smiled happily. He couldn't hear a word Papa said!

Make music

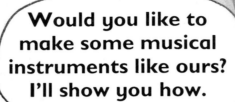

Shaker

> Would you like to make some musical instruments like ours? I'll show you how.

Wash and dry an empty yogurt pot.

Put a handful of dried peas, beans or small pasta shapes inside.

Put some cling film over the top. Keep it on with an elastic band.

Shake!

Cymbals

Hold a tin pan lid in each hand.

Crash them together!

Big bass drum

Hold a dustbin lid on one hand. A plastic one won't work. Or use a big pan.

Hit the lid or bottom of the pan hard with a big spoon.

Guitar

Find the lid of a biscuit tin.

Stretch 4 or 5 elastic bands across it.

Twang them with your fingers, like guitar strings.

Don't forget a conducting stick for the conductor. I used a fish bone, but you could use a chopstick!

15

Where is Grandpa?

The teacher took this photograph of the audience when the school orchestra was playing. A lot of parents and brothers and sisters came to listen. Can you see where Grandpa is sitting?

The answer is on page 61.

The ice caves

1. Pingu and Robby were playing together one day. "I'm really bored," said Pingu. "So am I," said Robby.

2. "Shall we go fishing?" asked Pingu. Robby shook his head. "No. What about skating?" Pingu shook HIS head.

3. Then Robby had an idea. "I know," he said. "Let's go to the ice caves." Pingu shook his head. "No, we're not allowed."

4. Robby felt naughty. "I'm going anyway," he said. "I don't care." Pingu thought for a minute. "I don't care either. Let's go."

17

5. They went inside Papa's shed. "This is just what we need," said Pingu. "A big torch. It's dark in the caves."

6. Pingu searched around for a bit until he found Papa's hard hat. He put it on. It was a bit big for him, but he didn't care.

7. "What about me?" Robby said. "I need a hard hat, too." Pingu had an idea. "Wait here," he said, and went into the igloo.

8. Pingu came out with Pinga's potty and put it on Robby's head. He had a warm scarf each, too. They set off for the ice caves.

9. The entrance to the ice caves was like a big black hole in the snow. "Come on, I'll lead the way," said Robby bravely.

10. The caves were cold and still and quiet. Pingu and Robby walked on and on. Soon they were deep, deep under the ground.

11. Suddenly the light from the torch grew dim. It flickered for a moment, then went out. It was very, very dark now.

12. "Turn the torch on!" said Robby. "I can't!" said Pingu. "It's not working. The batteries must have run out. Oh, what are we going to do now?"

19

13. Pingu and Robby hugged each other. It was very dark and they suddenly felt very frightened. "How can we find our way out?" said Pingu.

14. Pingu felt cold and started to shiver. "Someone will come and find us," said Robby. "But no one knows that we are down here!" said Pingu.

15. "Let's go this way," said Robby, but then he stopped. "Something is holding me back," he told Pingu. Pingu shivered even harder.

16. "It's my scarf," said Robby. "The wool is coming undone. It must be caught on something." Then he had an idea. "I wonder..." he said.

17. Robby took the wool in one flipper and Pingu's wing in the other. "If the wool is caught outside, we can follow it back," he said.

18. Slowly he led Pingu back through the dark, cold caves. It seemed to take a long time to walk. The ice caves didn't seem so exciting now.

19. Suddenly, Pingu grabbed Robby's flipper. "Look!" he said. "I can see a bit of light, Robby. We must be getting near to the entrance."

20. Soon they were outside. The wool was caught round a rock. "I'm never going in the ice caves again," said Pingu, "unless it's with Papa! Waark!"

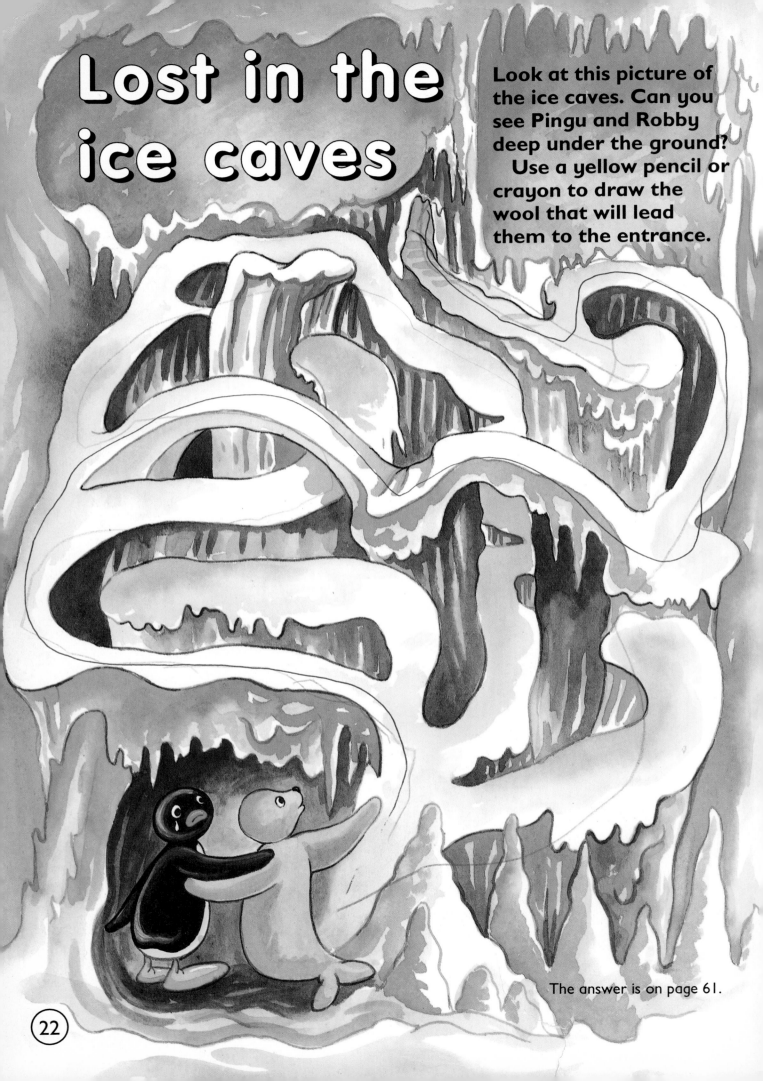

Lost in the ice caves

Look at this picture of the ice caves. Can you see Pingu and Robby deep under the ground?
Use a yellow pencil or crayon to draw the wool that will lead them to the entrance.

The answer is on page 61.

P is for Pingu

The answers are on page 61.

Make a Pingu badge

You will need:
a piece of card
scissors
felt-tip pens
sticky tape
a safety pin

1 Ask a grown up to help you cut out a piece of card the same shape and size as this one.

2 Draw Pingu's eyes on the card shape, like this:

Colour the middle parts black.

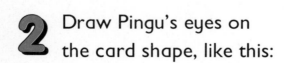

3 Now draw and colour his beak orange.

4 Colour his feathers black.

5 Turn the badge over. Tape a safety pin to the back.

A surprise for Grandpa

Mama, Pingu and Pinga were sitting at the table one Saturday morning, eating breakfast. They had a lot to talk about, and were busy making plans and whispering and laughing happily.

Grandpa came in carrying a newspaper. He looked happy. "Good morning," he said. "Nice day, isn't it?"

Mama, Pingu and Pinga stopped whispering as soon as Grandpa came in and pretended to be busy doing other things. Pinga finished her milk, Mama cleared the table and Pingu decided

to help with the washing up.

Grandpa sat down and opened the newspaper. "Hmm," he said. "Fourth of March, eh?"

Mama and Pingu had their backs to Grandpa. They giggled quietly, but didn't say anything. Pinga was still busy drinking her milk. She looked at Grandpa, but she didn't say anything, either.

Just then Papa came to the door with the post. Grandpa got up and rushed to him. "Lots of post for me today, I suppose?" he said.

Papa looked puzzled, and shook his head. "No, nothing for you today," he said. "Just a bill for us. Were you expecting something?"

Grandpa looked very unhappy. "Er, no, no, not really," he said. "I just thought that ... well, never mind, it's nothing." Grandpa sat down again and hid behind his newspaper.

Pinga didn't like to see Grandpa looking sad, and she rushed across to give him a big hug. She climbed up on to his knee and was just about to whisper something in his ear when Pingu caught her eye.

Pingu put his flipper over his beak and shook his head at Pinga. He didn't say anything – he didn't have to. Pingu meant, don't you dare say a word!

Pinga didn't say anything. Instead, she gave Grandpa a kiss on the cheek and clambered down on to the floor again.

Grandpa looked puzzled – what was going on?

Grandpa looked miserable all morning. Mama was too busy cooking to take any notice of him. Pingu didn't want to practise his accordion playing. Even Pinga didn't want to play monsters with him.

"I've got a lot to do this afternoon," Mama said to Grandpa after lunch. "Why don't you go out for a while? You could go for a walk."

Grandpa sighed. She's trying to get rid of me, he thought sadly. No one wants anything to do with me, today of all days. "Yes, all right," he said. "I don't want to be in the way."

"See you later," said Mama. "Tea will be at four o'clock. Don't be late."

Grandpa had a miserable day.

He walked to the post office, but the post master was too busy to talk to him and Papa was still out on his rounds.

He visited Professor Threehorn, but he was rushing off to buy something. He wouldn't let Grandpa go with him. He wouldn't even tell Grandpa what he was going to buy. "It's, well, a secret," said the professor.

"Oh," said Grandpa. "I see."

At four o'clock Grandpa walked back to the igloo and sat outside on a bench. He looked really fed up.

The door opened. "Time for tea, Grandpa!" called Mama.

Grandpa didn't feel hungry, and almost didn't go inside, but then he shrugged and stood up. "I suppose I may as well go inside," he said. "There's nothing else to do."

It was dark inside the igloo. "Eh!" said Grandpa. "What's going on?"

He soon found out. Suddenly the lights went on and he saw Mama, Papa, Pingu, the post master, Professor Threehorn and all his other friends.

"SURPRISE!" they all shouted at once. "HAPPY BIRTHDAY!"

Grandpa gasped. "I thought you had all forgotten my birthday," he said.

Pingu wheeled in a trolley with a huge cake on it. There were lots of candles burning on top – too many candles to count. "As if we would forget your birthday, Grandpa!" he said. "Happy birthday!"

Grandpa's gift

Professor Threehorn bought Grandpa a very special gift for his birthday. Join the dots to find out what it was.

The answer is on page 61.

50 SUPER PRIZES TO BE WON!

10 PINGU'S IGLOO PLAYSETS

10 TALKING PINGUS

10 WIND UP WALKING PINGUS

20 PLASTIC COLLECTABLES

HOW TO ENTER

It's easy! All you have to do is answer this simple question:

Who is Pingu's very best friend?

Write the answer on a postcard or envelope, with your name, age and address.

Send to:
Pingu Competition, Marketing Department, Egmont Publishing,
PO Box III, Great Ducie Street, Manchester M60 3BL.

Closing date: Ist February 1996.

The first 50 correct entries selected at random after the closing date will win a prize.

COMPETITION

A gift for Pinga

1. Mama was showing Pingu how to make papier-mache. They tore up bits of newspaper, dipped them in paste and moulded them round a balloon to make a bowl. Pingu loved it because it was very messy.

2. Pinga was not feeling very well and she was resting in bed. "I'm going to make something special for Pinga to cheer her up," Pingu told Mama. Mama asked what, but Pingu wouldn't say. "It's a secret!"

Sorting it out

Can you help Pingu and Pinga sort out their toys?
Which toys belong to Pingu and
which belong to Pinga?

The answers are on page 61.

How many penguins?

**Pingu and his friends are having fun in the playground.
How many penguins can you count?**

9 penguins

The answer is on page 61.

Sports day

Pingu and Robby like playing sports. One day they were playing outside the igloo when Papa came back from playing a game of curling with his friends from the Post Office.

"Can we have a game of curling, Papa?" Pingu asked.

"I haven't got time to play with you today," said Papa.

"I'm going to see Grandpa."

"You don't have to play," said Pingu. "We know the rules. We'll play by ourselves."

"Not with my curling stones you won't!" said Papa. "Now off you go."

"Waark!" said Pingu. "It's not fair!"

Then Pingu had an idea. "I know a sport we could try. I read about it in a book. It's called putting the shot. You get a really heavy ball thing and throw it. The one whose ball goes the furthest is the winner."

Robby nodded his head. He liked throwing things. "Good idea. We'll play putting the shot instead of curling," he said.

"No," said Pingu, who had just had another idea. "We're going to play putting the shot AND curling."

"But what about curling stones?" asked Robby. "We haven't got any, and Papa said you couldn't use his."

"We don't need his," said Pingu. "Look, you go and call for Ping and Pingo. I'll meet you near the fishing holes." Pingu pointed to the igloo. "I'm going to collect all the special things we'll need."

While Robby was away Pingu was busy. He read all the rules of curling then looked for Mama. She was busy outside, tidying all the bits and pieces in Papa's shed. "Good," said Pingu. "That will take ages."

Pingu went into the kitchen and took the lids from the pans. He took the biggest lids he could find. Then he opened the cupboard and searched inside for a while. He came out carrying Mama's big sweeping brush. Last of all he took the long tape measure from a drawer.

Pingu loaded the pan lids, brush and tape measure on to his sledge and rushed off to the fishing holes. Robby, Ping and Pingo were already there, waiting for him.

Pingu told his friends what to do. "Sweep this flat piece of ice until it's really smooth and shiny," he told Robby, handing him the brush. "Sweep off all the tiny stones and bits of ice. Ping and Pingo, you go up there and scratch a line across the ice with this sharp stone."

While his friends were busy Pingu rubbed the bottom edges of the pan lids with a stone to make them smooth.

When everything was ready Pingu explained the rules. "We will play in two teams. Ping and Pingo on one, Robby and me on the other. We take turns to push our lids along the icy course. They should go really fast now that the ice is smooth. The ones that get nearest to

the line up there are the winners."

"Easy," said Robby, and he hurled his pan lid along the course. But it didn't go straight and crashed into a rock. The same thing happened to Ping and Pingu's pan lids. Not one of them was anywhere near the line.

It was Pingo's turn next. He pushed his pan lid as hard as he could. It went straight towards the line until it hit a bit of ice Robby had not swept away and turned off to the left. With a loud *plop!* it disappeared into a fishing hole and slid under the water!

"Oh, no, the pan lid!" said Pingu.

"I'll get it," said Robby, and he dived into the water.

He was soon back, carrying the pan lid in his mouth. Pingu looked at the lid. It was battered and dented, and so were the other three when they found them. "Er, curling isn't much fun, is it?" asked Pingu. "Shall we try putting the shot instead?"

"Yes," said Ping. "What do we do?"

"Get some ice and snow and mould it into hard balls," said Pingu. "One each."

Pingu scratched a circle in the snow.

"You go first, Ping," said Pingu. "Stand inside the circle, then spin around and see how far you can throw the ball. Robby can measure the distances with the tape measure."

Ping spun around. He threw the ball of snow, but it was a lot heavier than it looked, and it didn't go far.

Neither did Pingo's. Pingu spun around as fast as he could, but his feet skidded on the ice and his shot landed with a plop in a deep pile of soft snow.

Robby was last to go. He was good at balancing things on his nose, so he put the shot on the tip of his nose, spun around and the shot flew though the air. It landed quite a long way away.

Robby didn't need to measure the distances the shots had gone. His shot had gone much further than the others.

"Waark!" said Pingu, who came last.

"That's not fair, you used your nose. It doesn't say anything about using your nose to put the shot in my book."

"Shall we play putting the shot again?" said Robby. "I like it."

Ping and Pingo wanted to play, but Pingu was fed up. "No, I'm going to take the pan lids home." He was starting to worry about how bashed they were. "See you tomorrow."

Pingu managed to get the pan lids, the brush and the tape measure into the igloo without Mama seeing him.

He was reading his sports book when Mama took the brush from the cupboard to brush the floor. "That's funny," she said. "How did the brush get all wet?"

Pingu said nothing.

Papa had a problem, too. He couldn't understand why the lids were all bent and wouldn't fit on the pans.

Pingu said nothing.

After supper Papa came to talk to Pingu, who was reading his sports book again. He was looking at the page about putting the shot. "These sports look interesting," said Papa. "Have you tried any of them?"

Pingu blushed. He didn't know what to say! "Er, I think I'll stick to skating," was all he could manage.

Which sport?

**Pingu can't decide which sport to play.
Can you match the things he is wearing
and holding to the list of sports?**

American football   rugby   cricket   tennis   hockey

The answers are on page 61.

Make a snowstorm shaker

I live at the South Pole, so I see snow all the time. You can, too, if you make a snowstorm shaker. I'll show you how. Ask a grown-up to help you.

You will need:
a small glass jar with a screw-on top
small plastic models or cake decorations – look for a penguin and an igloo!
silver glitter
glycerine – ask a grown-up to get some from a chemist
glue
water
teaspoon

1 Glue the models or cake decorations to the inside of the lid. Leave it to dry.

2 Put some glycerine into the glass jar. Fill the jar to the top with water. Look at the drawing to see how much of each.

3 Add a teaspoonful of glitter and stir it in.

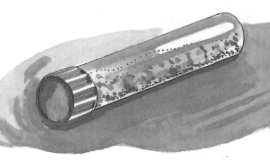

4 Screw the lid on to the glass jar. Turn it so that the lid is at the bottom. Shake it to make the snow fall.

Treasure trail

1. Pingu was working hard at the kitchen table one morning. He was writing on pieces of yellow paper and putting them into his school bag.

2. He was making a pirate treasure trail for his friends to follow. He was going to leave the paper clues for his friends to follow to find the treasure.

3. Earlier that morning Pingu had filled a box with chocolate pretend coins. He had buried it in the snow near the fishing holes.

4. "What are you doing, Pingu?" asked Pinga as her brother put the last of the paper clues into his shoulder bag. "What is in the bag?"

5. Pingu was in a hurry and he didn't want to be bothered with Pinga. "It's nothing for you," said Pingu. "Now go and play. I'm busy."

6. "I want to play with you," said Pinga. "Is it a new game?" Pingu was fed up with his sister. "It's not a game," he said. "Now GO AWAY!"

7. Pinga's eyes filled with tears and she went off to play with her toy piano. Pingu ignored her and put his bag on his shoulder.

8. Pingu set off from outside the igloo to lay his clues. He put the first one just beside the front door and the second one near Papa's shed.

9. Soon Pingu was far away from the igloo, busily laying his paper clues. Pinga came out of the igloo to play with her doll's pram.

10. Pinga saw a piece of paper near the door. She picked it up and looked at it. She couldn't read the words on the paper, but it looked important.

11. Pinga put the paper in her pram and wheeled her doll around. She found another piece of paper near Papa's shed. She put that in her pram, too.

12. By the time Pingu got back to the igloo Pinga was far way. His friends were waiting. "Look for paper clues to help you find the treasure," Pingu told them.

13. Robby, Ping, Pingi and Pingo searched and searched, but they could not find any of the clues. They didn't find any paper at all.

14. After an hour they went back to the igloo. "I suppose this is your idea of a joke, Pingu!" said Ping. Even Pingi looked angry with Pingu.

15. "What do you mean?" asked Pingu. Robby explained. "The clues," he said. "There aren't any!" Pingo agreed. "That's right," he said. "Not one."

16. Pingu decided to check. He went to the side of the door where he had put the first clue. It was not there. Neither was the clue near Papa's shed.

17. Where were the clues? Who had taken them? All Pingu could do was shrug. "I don't know what has happened," he said. His friends went home, fed up.

18. Later, when Papa came home he was carrying a big envelope full of pieces of paper. "Look what I found in the post box," he said. Pingu's paper clues!

19. "They are my treasure trail clues," said Pingu. "But how did they get in the post box?" Pinga tapped Pingu's flipper. She looked very pleased with herself.

20. "Pinga found letters," said Pinga. "Took them to post box in my doll's pram. Pinga posted them!" "Oh, no!" said Pingu, but he couldn't help laughing.

Sharing

Sharing is important. Do you share with your friends? You can share books and toys. You can share ideas as well. You can share happy things, like jokes. You can share sad things, like something you might be worried about.

Think about the treasure trail story. Did Pingu share his plans for the treasure trail with Pinga? No, he didn't, even though she asked him to. If he had shared his plans she wouldn't have spoiled the game by picking up the paper clues, would she? It's good to share.

Pingu caught lots of fish one day. He wanted to share them with his friends Robby and Pingi. There were 6 fish. How many each for Robby, Pingi and Pingu?

The answers are on page 61.

Make a Pingu puppet

You will need:
2 white paper plates
sticky tape
black, red and yellow felt-tip
pens or crayons

This Pingu puppet is easy to make.
Ask a grown-up to help you.

52

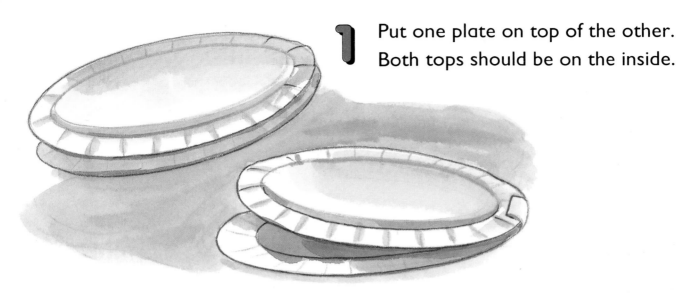

1 Put one plate on top of the other. Both tops should be on the inside.

2 Hold the plates together with pieces of sticky tape. Leave a gap at the bottom.

3 Draw Pingu's eyes and beak on one plate. Colour it.

4 Colour the back of his head black.

That's it! Slip your hand in the gap at the bottom to move your Pingu puppet.

You could make a Robby puppet in the same way, and put on a puppet show.

Pingu goes shopping

Pingu gets some spending money each week. He calls it 'spends'.
 Do you get spends? What do you like to buy?

Pingu gets 10p from Mama and Papa.

Pingu likes to buy things with his spends.

On Saturday morning he went shopping.

Pingu bought a bar of chocolate for 4p.

What can he buy with the money he has left?

Has he enough money to buy a comic and a toy car? yes

The answers are on page 61.

Laughs with Pingu

"I'm frightened!"

Papa looked at the clock on the wall. It was seven o'clock. "Come on, Pingu," said Papa. "It's time for bed. Pinga is already fast asleep."

Pingu was reading a book about dinosaurs. "Can I just finish this page please?" he asked.

"All right," said Papa.

But five minutes later Pingu still didn't want to go to bed. "Can I just put the book in my school bag for tomorrow?" he asked.

"If you're quick," said Papa.

Pingu was just about to get into bed when he stopped. "Can I just have a drink of milk?" he asked.

Papa brought a glass of milk, kissed Pingu and said goodnight. Mama came in to say goodnight, too. When she had kissed Pingu and given him a big hug she reached out to turn off the bedside light. But Pingu stopped her. "Leave the light on, Mama, please. PLEASE!" he said.

"But you don't usually have the light on, Pingu," said Mama.

"I know, but I want it on tonight, Mama," said Pingu. "I'm frightened!"

"What are you frightened of?" asked Mama.

"I had a bad dream," said Pingu. "I don't like the dark now. I'm frightened."

Mama cuddled Pingu again. "There's nothing to be frightened of," she told him. She left the light on as Pingu had asked, and soon he was fast asleep.

The same thing happened every night. Pingu just would not go to sleep without the bedside light on.

Mama was a little bit worried, and told Grandpa about it. "I just can't make Pingu understand that there is nothing to be frightened of in the dark," she said. "I don't want him to feel scared."

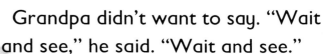

Grandpa thought for a minute. "I think I might be able to help," he said.

"How?" asked Mama.

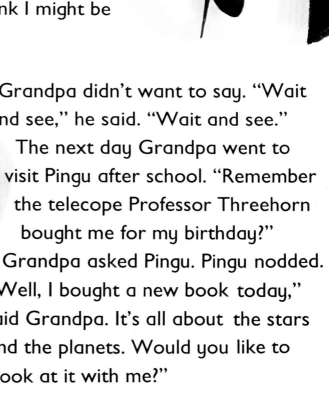

Grandpa didn't want to say. "Wait and see," he said. "Wait and see."

The next day Grandpa went to visit Pingu after school. "Remember the telecope Professor Threehorn bought me for my birthday?" Grandpa asked Pingu. Pingu nodded. "Well, I bought a new book today," said Grandpa. It's all about the stars and the planets. Would you like to look at it with me?"

"Yes, please," said Pingu.

Grandpa and Pingu spent ages looking at the book. Pingu really liked it. He tried to remember the names of all the planets.

When they had looked at the last page Grandpa took a sheet of yellow paper from his bag. "Let's draw some star and planet shapes and cut them out, shall we?" said Grandpa.

When they had made lots of shapes Pingu said, "Shall we stick them on a piece of paper?"

Grandpa had a better idea. "Let's stick them to the ceiling over your bed," he told Pingu. "This paper is special. It's called luminous paper, which means that it shines in the dark. When you look up at the shapes it will be just like looking at the real stars and planets in the sky at night."

Grandpa stood on a chair and Pingu held it while Grandpa stuck the paper stars and planets on the ceiling.

After supper Pingu couldn't wait for bedtime. He jumped into bed and looked up. But Pingu was disappointed. "The shapes don't look very good," he grumbled. "I can't see them very well."

Grandpa knew why. "It's because the shapes are made of special paper. It only glows in the dark. We need the room to be really dark to see them well. Shall I turn the bedside light off?"

Pingu wasn't sure. "I don't know," he told Grandpa. "I don't like the dark. It's scary. I like to keep the light on."

"But I'll stay here with you," said Grandpa. "I'll sit here on the edge of the bed. You can hold my flippers. How about that?"

Pingu still wasn't sure, but he DID want to see the stars and planets shining in the dark.

He thought for a moment. "All right, you can turn the light off," he said at last. "But stay with me, won't you, Grandpa?"

"Of course I will," said Grandpa.

Grandpa switched off the lamp and he and Pingu

looked up at the dark ceiling. The stars and
planets glowed and shone. "They look just
like the real ones do through my telescope,"
said Grandpa.

"Which is the biggest planet?" asked Pingu. "And
the hottest one?" He didn't mind about being in the
dark now. He wasn't frightened. Being in the dark was
interesting. "How many stars are there altogether?" he
asked. "What are they made of?"

Grandpa laughed. "One question at a time, please!" he said.

He told Pingu all about the planets and the stars until he
heard a soft purring sort of a sound.

Pingu had fallen asleep and was snoring quietly.

"Goodnight, Pingu," whispered Grandpa. "Sweet dreams."

Answers to puzzles

Page 8 **What is different?**

Page 16 **Where is Grandpa?**

Page 22 **Lost in the ice caves**

Page 23 **P is for Pingu**

page 30 **Grandpa's gift**
Grandpa's gift was a telescope.

Page 36 **Sorting it out**
Pingu has a trumpet, a paintbox and a teddy. Pinga has a doll's pram, a pull-along duck and a balloon.

Page 37 **How many penguins?**
There are 9 penguins.

Page 43 **Which sport?**
American football – shirt and helmet
rugby – ball
cricket – bat
tennis – racquet
hockey – stick

Page 51 **Sharing**
Robby, Pingi and Pingu get 2 fish each.

Page 54 **Pingu goes shopping**
Yes, Pingu has enough money to buy a comic and a toy car.